Bantam Books in the Choose Your Own Adventure® series
Ask your bookseller for the books you have missed

SCENE OF THE CRIME

BY DOUG WILHELM

ILLUSTRATED BY TOM LA PADULA

An R.A. Montgomery Book

BANTAM BOOKS

NEW YORK · TORONTO · LONDON · SYDNEY · AUCKLAND

RL4, age 10 and up

SCENE OF THE CRIME

A Bantam Book/July 1993

CHOOSE YOUR OWN ADVENTURE® is a registered
trademark of Bantam Books, a division of Bantam Doubleday
Dell Publishing Group, Inc. Registered in U.S. Patent and
Trademark Office and elsewhere.

Original conception of Edward Packard
Cover art by Bill Dodge
Interior illustrations by Tom La Padula

ISBN 0-553-56004-2

Published simultaneously in the United States and Canada

Bantam Books are published by Bantam Books, a division of Bantam
Doubleday Dell Publishing Group, Inc. Its trademark, consisting of the
words "Bantam Books" and the portrayal of a rooster, is Registered in
U.S. Patent and Trademark Office and in other countries. Marca Regis-
trada. Bantam Books, 1540 Broadway, New York, New York 10036.

PRINTED IN THE UNITED STATES OF AMERICA

OPM   0 9 8 7 6 5 4 3 2 1

For Christopher Wilhelm

<u>**WARNING!!!**</u>

Do not read this book straight through from beginning to end. These pages contain many different adventures that you may have as you try to get to the bottom of a conspiracy brewing in your peaceful home town. From time to time as you read along, you'll have a chance to make a choice. Your choice may lead to success or disaster!

The adventures you have are the results of your choices. You are responsible because you choose. After you make your decision, follow the instructions to find out what happens to you next.

Think carefully before you act. The people you're up against are ruthless, and they'll do almost anything to make sure their plans are carried out. You're the only one who knows what they're up to, but can you stop them? If you try, you'll have to be ready for anything—bribery, kidnapping, even murder!

Good luck!

Summer is almost over, and you've just returned home from a six-week visit with your grandparents. It was a lot of fun, but you're glad to get back to Grantshire, Vermont, your hometown. The morning after you get home, you ride your bike out to the big empty lot at the edge of town. To most folks in Grantshire, it's just a raggedy stretch of grass and trees. But you and your friends call it the old ballpark. You know its hiding places and its secret trails, and you know the open field where base paths have been worn through the weedy grass by years of kids playing ball.

Your imagination has turned the old lot into the scene of many childhood adventures, from Fenway Park, home of your beloved Boston Red Sox, to the wild jungles of the Amazon, to a tropical island rich with pirate gold.

But when you ride up to the lot, you get a terrible shock. Staring you in the face is a large sign:

COMING SOON AT THIS SITE—
MAPLE GROVE MALL
NINETY-SEVEN STORES!
NO TRESPASSING

Turn to page 2.

2

You can't believe your eyes. You turn your bike around and pedal fast to the office of Hornbeck Real Estate, where your mother works. When you run inside, she's talking on the phone. But when she sees your face, she hangs up immediately.

"What is it?" she asks you.

"Mom, they're going to bulldoze our ballpark!"

"Oh, I'm sorry, honey. I should have told you," she says. "But just think, a big indoor mall! You know, your friends are pretty excited about it."

You shrug. "Yeah, I guess that could be cool. But why do they have to build it on our ballpark?"

A few blocks away, you find your best friends, Corey and Kate, sitting on Corey's front porch.

Corey jumps up and smiles when he sees you. "Hey, welcome home!"

"Hi guys," you say. "Did you hear about the new mall?"

"It's going to be great," says Kate. "I bet it'll have a big electronics store."

"And a video arcade and a record store and a pizza place," Corey adds. "At last—somewhere decent to hang out."

"I guess so," you say. "But I wish they'd picked a different place to build it."

Go on to the next page.

"Hey, these guys do whatever they want to wherever they want to." Corey shrugs. "It's not safe to get in their way."

"What do you mean?" you ask.

Corey hands you a copy of the *Grantshire Observer,* the local weekly newspaper. "Read this."

You take the paper from him, and the headline catches your eye. It reads:

TOWN COUNCILMAN DISAPPEARS
FRANK SORRELL WAS MALL'S LONE OPPONENT

Turn to page 4.

4

You scan the article and learn that the Grantshire town council is about to decide whether to give the Maple Grove Mall project the go-ahead. The only council member who was against it was Frank Sorrell, a retired New York City police detective. But last week Sorrell went on a two-day fishing trip, and he hasn't come back.

"At this point, police do not suspect foul play," the newspaper reports. "But the councilman's daughter, New York attorney Andrea Sorrell, is reportedly coming to Grantshire to investigate."

Turn to page 25.

Lew Millman, of the *Grantshire Observer,* interviews you about your role in breaking the story. "How does it feel to be a hero?" he asks, putting down his notebook and picking up a camera.

"Aw, I don't know . . ." You shrug. Millman's flash goes off.

And that's the picture—you shrugging, looking goofy—that appears on the front page of the next *Grantshire Observer.*

The End

6

You follow Andrea into the darkened building. Your pen-sized flashlights throw little disks of light on the walls. You find the main office, a small room with a window overlooking the loading area. The office contains a single battered file cabinet. Andrea drops to her knees and starts to rummage through the files. You hope she finds something—quickly.

Instead she curses softly. "These files are a mess," she says.

"Andrea," you say. "Look at this."

You've noticed a large wall map showing this part of Vermont. Certain roads have been highlighted in pink, yellow, and green marker. They lead from Grantshire to Burlington, Montpelier, Middlebury, and other Vermont cities and towns —and also off to New York State, Canada, and New Hampshire.

"It's Belleville's route map," Andrea whispers.

"Right," you say. "Now look at this."

Turn to page 14.

You wake up in a hospital bed. Your head hurts like crazy, and your left shoulder is heavily bandaged. You can't move it, and it hurts too. So do your ribs.

Your mother is sitting by your bed. She puts down her newspaper when you open your eyes.

"Oh thank heavens," she says. "You're awake!"

"Mom . . . what happened?"

"Some kind of hit-and-run—a car hit you from behind, and knocked you into a tree. Your shoulder and chest took a lot of the impact, but your head smacked that tree pretty hard. You've had a serious concussion, and you broke your shoulder and two ribs. You've been unconscious for three days."

"Three days?" you repeat slowly.

"Incredible, isn't it? But look. The newspaper doesn't lie."

The date on the *Grantshire Observer* says Thursday—three days after the town council meeting. And the headline reads:

MAPLE GROVE MALL WILL BE BUILT

"I can't believe that hit-and-run driver didn't stop," your mother continues. "The police say they don't have any clues. The doctors say you're lucky to be alive."

You lie back against the pillows and close your eyes. "I think they're right," you answer quietly.

The End

Both cars' lights are off, but both engines remain running. You notice that both cars have radio antennas with odd, squiggly things in the middle that look like sections of notebook spiral.

You hear a *whirr* as the dark car's push-button window lowers.

The driver of the white car cranks down his window. You can just see his face, and you recognize him as town councilman Art Collins.

Collins talks cheerfully, in a gravelly voice. Trying to hear better, you crawl very slowly out along the tree's lowest branch. You lie very still, hugging the branch as you listen.

"We're getting close," you hear Collins say. "It's all gonna pay off."

"Good," says a man's voice from the dark car. "Because it has to."

Now a hand emerges from the dark car. It holds a thick manila envelope. Councilman Collins takes the envelope and nods.

"We'll do this one more time, right?" says Collins. "The night after the vote. That'll be the big payment."

"Yes," says the other voice. "We'll make the connection in the same way."

Collins rolls up his window and drives out of the parking lot.

The dark car waits a few minutes. Then it leaves too.

Turn to page 46.

The next morning you head for the office of the *Grantshire Observer,* which is in a weather-beaten wood building on a side street off Coolidge Avenue, the main street in town. Inside the office, a mound of papers nearly covers a desk, a computer, and a man who is losing his hair.

The man blinks at you. "Hi," he says. "What can I do for you?"

"I'm looking for the editor."

"I'm Lew Millman, the editor," he says. "Also the reporter, the layout artist, and the ad salesman." He smiles. "The *Observer*'s a pretty small paper."

You tell Lew Millman what you saw behind the Grantshire Market, and that you suspect the town council is being bribed to approve the Maple Grove Mall. "So you can investigate," you finish. "Right?"

But the editor shakes his head. "I'm sorry," he says. "The town council is going to vote on the mall project at seven o'clock tonight. The next issue of the paper doesn't come out until Thursday. Even if I had time to do some kind of investigation—which I'm afraid I don't—it would be too late to make a difference."

Turn to page 94.

"That's a terrific idea," says Collins. "Let me tell you, this mall is going to be heaven for young people. It'll be full of great stuff. You know what I'm saying?"

"What kinds of great stuff?" you ask.

"Oh, like a pizza parlor, a video arcade, a record store, three discount fashion outlets—I can't even remember everything. We—I mean, they—are even thinking of building a skateboarding area in the parking lot."

"A skateboarding area? That's unusual. Could you tell me more about it?"

"Sure," says Collins. "The people who are building this mall are very interested in attracting young people. And that means skateboards. So rather than have skateboarding be a problem . . ."

You cover the phone with your palm. "He's a real talker," you whisper. Corey nods and rolls his eyes. As Collins talks on, you both watch the homemade box with the flashlight bulb. A couple of questions and long answers later, the bulb finally flicks on. Corey gives you a thumbs-up. You know the light means that Kate has picked up Collins's frequency.

Turn to page 96.

After leaving the newspaper office, you hop on your bike and try to decide what to do next.

You could ride straight to the Grantshire police station and tell the chief what you saw last night. Or you could try to get the evidence that Lew Millman says you need. But how?

If you go to the police, turn to page 53.

If you try to get the evidence yourself, turn to page 22.

Several of the Belleville Transport routes marked on the map converge at a tiny spot in the country, a place called Woodard's Mill about thirty miles from Grantshire.

"What's that?" Andrea asks.

You shrug. "A tiny little town," you say. "Why would the trucks go there?"

Andrea shrugs. "When you need information," she says, "first try the obvious source." She grabs a local phone book that's lying on top of the filing cabinet. She thumbs through it. Then she stops. "Aha," she says.

"What?" you ask, peering over her shoulder.

"Look."

Turn to page 48.

You've found the right map in the *Vermont Atlas*. You study it with your penlight. "Okay," you say to Andrea. "Go down Route 7 to Newcomb Crossing, then turn east on 74. Woodard's Mill isn't far down. And I see Devil's Ditch Road here on the map."

"You're the navigator," says Andrea.

She pushes the car to fifty, the speed limit on Vermont two-lane highways. Now the powerful vehicle surges to sixty, then seventy. Soon you're doing seventy-five miles per hour.

"Andrea," you say, "what if we get stopped? I don't trust the Grantshire cops."

"That truck has a head start," she says. "Your friend's life may be at stake, and my father's. But you live around here—you know these roads. If you think we're likely to get stopped, I'll slow down. If you agree with me that it's worth the risk, I'll just get us there as fast as I can."

If you tell her to stick to the speed limit, turn to page 59.

If you tell her to keep speeding, turn to page 68.

16

You decide to try to talk to Strassen. The council meeting starts at 7:00 P.M. You, Corey, and Kate arrive outside the town hall at twenty before seven. You stand in the shadows beside the building, waiting for the long, dark car.

"He's not coming," says Corey at five before seven.

"Of course he is," says Kate. "It's his job to make sure this mall deal is approved."

"Look!" you whisper suddenly. Strassen's long black car is turning into the parking area. "That's the one," you say.

The car door opens, and a blond-haired man in a dark suit steps out. "Quick," Corey says. "Do we approach him in the parking lot, or wait until he goes inside?"

If you approach Strassen immediately, turn to page 112.

If you follow him inside and speak with him there, turn to page 110.

When you get home you tell your mother about what you saw behind the supermarket.

"Mom, you believe me. Right?"

"Of course I do," she says. "But how do you know that what you saw was something bad? That envelope could have had any number of things in it."

"But they talked about the *next payment*. That's what they said."

She looks closely at you. "Are you sure you're not just upset about losing your old ballpark?"

"What? You don't believe me either?"

"Now calm down," she says. "I know how much you love that place, but this mall will bring a lot of business to our town. So please—try not to let your imagination run away with you."

The grown-ups don't believe you. Your best friends think the mall is going to be great. This is getting kind of lonely. Maybe you should just forget about what you saw.

But then again, you might be the only one who knows the truth. It's not too late to go to the town council meeting. You can stand up and tell the council what you saw—and hope that *they'll* believe you.

If you go to the council meeting,
turn to page 30.

If you stay home,
turn to page 41.

Late that night, dressed in dark clothes, you and Corey lead Andrea along a path through the woods near Belleville Transport. When you reach the edge of the lot, you hold up your hand. Corey and Andrea come up behind you. You point ahead to a square, one-story building.

The trucking depot is silent. The paved lot around it is edged by an old wire fence. At this spot the dirt beneath the fence has been dug out. As kids you used to sneak into the Belleville lot sometimes just for fun. The three of you crawl under and then stand up on the other side.

"One of you stay out here as a lookout," Andrea whispers. "The other one come with me."

Corey looks at you. "Which do you want to do?"

If you stay outside as the lookout, turn to page 42.

If you go with Andrea, turn to page 45.

The councilman smiles calmly. "Why, no," he says. "I was home last night. Couldn't have been me."

"Oh," you say. "But it was a white car, just like this one."

Collins smiles again. "Oh, this old baby's a pretty ordinary car. Must be a dozen like it right in this town. Now listen—you just go right into that market and ask for an application. I'm sure a young person like you will get a job—if you're not just a little *too* young for that sort of thing." He looks at you closely.

"Well, ah, maybe. Anyway, I'm sorry to have bothered you."

"No bother at all."

Rats, you think as you walk back to your bike. As you start to ride out of the parking lot, you glance back at the white car. Collins is talking again on his car phone, looking very agitated.

And he's looking right at you.

Something tells you it's time to ride home— fast. A few minutes later you're pedaling hard and breathing heavily. You hear a car coming up fast behind you. You turn a corner and hear the car turn it too.

No one else is around. Scared to look back, you ride as hard as you can. But the car is speeding up—you hear a *whoosh* as it comes up behind you.

Suddenly you feel yourself flying through the air. And that's the last thing you remember.

Turn to page 8.

The police will never believe you. You decide to enlist your friends' help instead. You call your mother and tell her that you're going to Kate's house for dinner.

Actually there's no time for dinner, but you are going to Kate's. You have an idea, and you're going to need her help. Luckily for you, Kate's deeply into gadgetry.

"What's up?" says Kate when she answers her door.

"Kate, if you wanted to secretly tape a conversation, how would you do it?"

Your friend's eyes narrow.

"You've been acting a little weird since you got back," she says. "What's going on?"

You quickly tell her the whole story.

"Wow," she says when you've finished. "What's your plan?"

"I need evidence," you say. "So if Councilman Collins should happen to say something that proves he was behind the supermarket last night, and if I should happen to record what he says . . ."

"I'd call that evidence," Kate finishes.

You nod. "The council meeting starts at seven tonight. If I get there a little early, I can try to have a short chat with Councilman Collins beforehand. I just need you to fix me up with the equipment."

"You came to the right place," Kate says with a grin.

Turn to page 85.

A few minutes later, as you and Corey are riding past the old ballpark, you hear another car coming up fast behind you. But you never even have time to turn to see if it's the dark car.

The entire community is shocked when the news of the drive-by shooting gets out. Nothing like it has ever happened in Grantshire before.

The End

You spend the rest of the day thinking about the mall. You wonder if it's possible that the mall developers took Frank Sorrell out of the way. You can't believe that that kind of thing could happen in Grantshire.

Later that evening you head back to Corey's house. You want to talk this over with him.

You decide to take the secret shortcut to his yard. You cut through the Grantshire Market's parking lot. The supermarket is closed. You climb a chain link fence at the back of the lot then swing onto the overhanging branch of the big old apple tree in Corey's backyard.

You're about to jump down from the tree into the yard when a long, dark car with its headlights off comes around the back corner of the supermarket. You stop and watch as the car comes to a stop a few feet below your perch. Its motor is running.

A moment later a second car, a battered white sedan, pulls up beside the first car.

Turn to page 9.

"Sure," says Millman. "The big-city firm that wants to build the mall is called the Cairo Corporation. The people who run it are rich and powerful—some say they're ruthless. Their local agent is Gil Strassen. You may have seen him around. Blond-haired guy, wears nice suits."

"He drives that big black car," you say, trying to sound casual. "Right?"

"That's him," says Millman. "But he doesn't like reporters—thinks we can't be trusted. You can try him, but I think your best source is a town councilman named Art Collins."

You, Corey, and Kate trade glances.

"For some reason, Collins is a very big supporter of this mall," Millman says. "He's been pulling for it all along. The council is voting on it tonight, by the way. Now, Art loves to talk. He works as a salesman—just about lives in his car. He calls everyone on his cellular phone."

Millman's last words have given you an idea. "Okay," you say, "we'll get started. Thanks!" You hustle Corey and Kate away.

"Uh, sure," Millman calls after you. "Call me if you need anything."

"Kate," you say when you're out of earshot. "Does a little squiggle on a car antenna have anything to do with a cellular phone?"

Go on to the next page.

"Sure," she says. "Only a cellular phone's car antenna has that squiggle. Why?"

"Both Collins's and Strassen's cars had them. When they said they'd talk again *in the usual way,* maybe they meant by car phone!"

Kate changes direction. "Follow me," she says.

"Where are we going?"

"Radio Cave."

Turn to page 87.

28

The next morning you pick up Corey and head for Frank Sorrell's house, hoping to talk to his daughter Andrea. About halfway there you stop your bike at a red light. A long black car pulls up beside you. It's the one that was at the secret rendezvous!

"Corey, we've got to follow that car," you say.

When the light changes, the car cruises ahead and turns onto a road leading out of town. You and Corey ride as hard as you can down the road after it, but you lose sight of it after a few seconds.

"Let's keep going a little farther," you suggest.

When you round a bend down the road you spot the car parking in the yard of a small local trucking company called Belleville Transport. You and Corey pull your bikes off the road behind a maple tree and watch as a slim, blond-haired man in a gray suit steps out of the dark car. He walks into the Belleville Transport office at one corner of the square, one-story building.

"What's he doing here?" you whisper.

"I don't know," Corey answers. "Maybe they kidnapped Sorrell and threw him into a truck."

You look over at your friend. "Corey," you whisper, "that's not such a crazy idea."

Suddenly you're grabbed from behind.

Turn to page 107.

You have to try to convince the town council of what you saw. It may be your only chance to stop the conspiracy.

That evening you get on your bike and head downtown. When you turn the corner at the end of your street, you pass a police car parked at the curb. You wonder what it's doing there.

You get to the town hall at a few minutes past seven. Hoping you've arrived in time, you park your bike and rush into the building. You even forget to be nervous—until you step into the meeting room, that is. When you push open the double doors, twenty or thirty people turn to look at you. You freeze.

Turn to page 63.

A few minutes later, the council votes six to nothing to approve the Maple Grove Mall. The meeting drones on, but you and your friends get up quietly and leave. Outside, you stop to plan your next move.

"So can anyone talk at a government meeting like that?" Corey asks.

"Sure," you say. "That's what it's all about."

"That's what it's *supposed* to be about," says Kate. "It makes me mad that someone's money can make a difference in secret."

"They'll go to jail for it if we catch them," you say. "So now what?"

"Strassen won't give us an inch," Corey says. "I say we try the Collins plan—get him talking on his car phone."

"I hope it works," you say as you get on your bike.

Turn to page 90.

You glance behind you to make sure that the chief's cruiser is gone. Then you and Corey continue to watch as the blond-haired man gets back into his car. With a soft crunch of gravel, the vehicle pulls out of Belleville's gate and turns down the road toward town. You and Corey flatten yourselves to the ground as the car glides by.

"Do you think he saw us?" Corey whispers.

"I don't think so," you say. "He was driving too fast."

"Let's follow him," says Corey.

"I don't know," you say slowly. "It could be risky. Maybe we should just head to Sorrell's house."

Corey shrugs. "It's up to you," he says. "I think we should go for it."

If you follow the dark car,
turn to page 69.

If you ride to Sorrell's house,
turn to page 40.

You and Corey ride hard as far as the railroad bridge at the edge of Grantshire. You drag your bikes down beneath the bridge and face each other. Corey looks scared, and you can't blame him—you are, too.

"That guy looked mean," Corey says. "And he got a really good look at us."

"How do you think he knew we were tailing him?"

"It had to be the chief," Corey says. "The chief must have called him somehow and told him. Then that guy must have pulled off the road to let us ride by, so he could come up behind us like that."

"He was probably just trying to scare us," you say.

"Well, he succeeded," says Corey. "Plus, he got a good look at both of us."

"So what? We haven't done anything wrong."

"No," says Corey. "But we'd better move very carefully from now on."

"Let's head to Sorrell's."

"Are you sure?"

"Why not? Those are public streets out there."

Turn to page 23.

You and Andrea get out of the car and lean against it as the police officer checks you for weapons.

"I'm an attorney, officer," Andrea says. "What's the charge?"

"You're suspected in a breaking and entering at Belleville Transport," the officer answers curtly.

He pulls your hands behind your back. You feel cold metal on your wrists as the handcuffs click shut.

Because you're a juvenile, you are released later that night. Toward morning, Corey is found walking on a lonely road not far from Woodard's Mill.

Andrea Sorrell is held for forty-eight critical hours. The police say the district court judge is on vacation, and another judge can't be found to set bail. Andrea is furious but helpless.

When she finally gets out, she calls the Vermont state police and insists that the Belleville warehouse in Woodard's Mill be searched. An officer drives over but finds nothing.

Frank Sorrell's body is never found.

The End

Sitting in Frank Sorrell's kitchen, you tell Andrea what you saw behind the Grantshire Market.

"It must have been someone from the Cairo Corporation," Andrea says grimly. "They're the mall developers. They build these things all over the country. They'll bulldoze anything and anyone that gets in their way. That's why I'm so worried about my dad."

"There's one more thing," you say. You tell her about the dark car stopping at Belleville Transport.

"Hmm," she says. "Wait here a minute." She goes upstairs.

A few minutes later, she comes back down. "I just called the town clerk," she tells you and Corey. "Belleville Transport was bought by Cairo Corporation just last month."

Turn to page 98.

You decide you have to wait. If you alone witness the payoff again, you'll have no more evidence than you already have.

The wavering lights are coming closer. You can see that Kate and Corey are breathing hard, pedaling as fast as they can.

You look toward the ballpark, but you can't really see what's happening. Strassen's headlights are off, just as they were behind Grantshire Market.

Your friends pull up. Gasping, Corey says, "Where?"

"Down there. Come on!"

But Kate is doubled over, panting. "I can't," she chokes out.

"You've got to!"

"I can't! Just hang on a second." She straightens up, holding her stomach. "Okay," she says. "Where are they?"

"At the ballpark."

Corey sits up straight. "You're kidding. Kate, get the camera ready."

"You take it," she tells you. "I couldn't hold it steady."

She hands you the camera. The flash's ready light glows orange. You turn and head toward the ballpark. But ahead you see some small red lights suddenly come on. Strassen's car pulls forward and drives away. The man on foot turns and walks quickly down the street.

"Oh, no," you sigh.

Turn to page 114.

Later that night you, Corey, and Kate are at the old ballpark, dressed in black. Each of you grips your piece of equipment as you crouch behind some bushes along the edge of the lot.

At two minutes before eleven a black car cruises up Coolidge Avenue and turns right onto Parson Street. It noses toward the sidewalk and stops on the other side of the bushes you're hiding behind. Corey slowly raises his microphone.

A man comes striding up Parson Street and stops beside the black car. It's Councilman Collins. The driver's window whirs down, and you recognize Gil Strassen inside.

"Mission accomplished," Collins says.

"Good job," says Strassen. He holds out a thick manila envelope. "Here's the final payment."

"Twenty thousand?"

"It's all there."

At the moment Collins takes the envelope, you hop up and press the shutter button. The flash catches both men looking at the camera, startled, their hands on the envelope.

You and your friends turn and run for your lives.

Turn to page 100.

You convince Corey to forget about the dark car and continue on to Frank Sorrell's house. When you get there, you're not too surprised to see a Grantshire police car parked just up the street.

"Ride past the house," you say to Corey. "Act natural."

He nods. The two of you pass the cruiser and round a corner. Then you stop, and Corey pulls up beside you.

"I don't think we want the Grantshire police to know we're visiting Andrea Sorrell," you say.

"No problem," says Corey. "I know this neighborhood like the back of my hand. Follow me."

He slides his bike into some bushes, glances right and left, and disappears between two houses.

Turn to page 108.

You decide not to bother. Why put yourself through it? Nobody will believe you anyway. You wander into the den to watch TV.

Three days later, the *Grantshire Observer* comes out. The headline says:

MAPLE GROVE MALL WILL BE BUILT

With Frank Sorrell absent, the Maple Grove Mall was approved unanimously. The article adds that there's still no news about the missing councilman.

With the paper in your lap, you sit on your front porch, wondering if you did the right thing.

The End

"I'll stay out here," you say.

Corey and Andrea nod. "Give a whistle if you see anything suspicious," Andrea tells you. Then she and Corey hurry across the lot to the building. When they reach the back door, you see Andrea take out a small hacksaw and cut through the padlock. Then she and Corey slip inside and disappear from your sight.

The night is quiet. A half moon casts a pale shimmer of light across the lot. A single Belleville truck stands idle near the building.

Suddenly everything goes dark. Someone has pulled a thick cloth over your face. A strong arm has your arms pinned to your side. You struggle vainly to escape as you're dragged away. After a moment you feel gravel under your flailing feet, and you hear a metal door roll up. You're tossed roughly onto a cold metal floor. The door rolls down, an engine starts, and with a jerk, you're moving.

You've been kidnapped!

Turn to page 62.

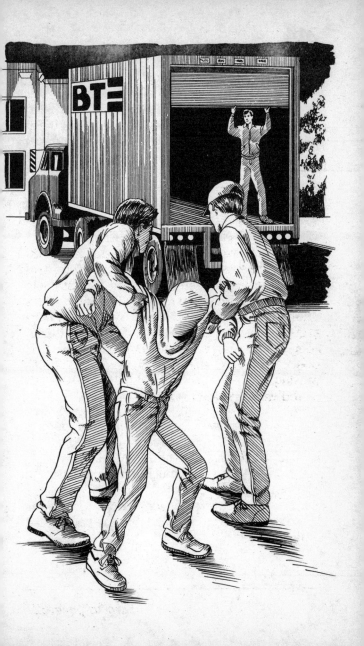

Following your directions, Andrea pulls off at a culvert where a stream passes beneath Devil's Ditch Road, about forty yards below the warehouse. She leaves her engine running and her lights off. The dense woods all around make it impossible to see the warehouse from her car.

You and Corey pick your way up the stream. The sound of running water covers your approach as you make your way to a point where you can see both downstream to Andrea and upstream to the warehouse.

Corey stays there. In his pocket is one of the penlights. The other is in your pocket, along with your pocketknife.

Ten minutes later, you're crawling up the bank of the stream. Peering over the edge, you see a low, rectangular building of corrugated metal—the Belleville warehouse.

A lone Belleville truck is backed up to the loading dock. A man is standing by the front bumper, peering up and down the road. You can hear someone moving around inside the warehouse. Otherwise there is only the gurgling sound of water in the stream behind you.

The man by the truck is watching the road. You don't know how much time you have. Got to move quickly.

You creep over the edge of the bank—and with a few steps, you make it to the back wall of the warehouse.

Turn to page 64.

"I'll go in with you," you say to Andrea.

"All right," she replies. "Corey, you stay here and keep a lookout for anything suspicious. Give a whistle if you see anything."

"Okay," Corey replies. "Good luck in there."

You and Andrea head for the building, moving as quickly and quietly as possible. You notice that there is only one truck parked in Belleville Transport's darkened lot. You hold your breath while Andrea takes out a small hacksaw and cuts open the padlock on the building's back door. You wait for an alarm, but you don't hear anything.

Turn to page 6.

46

Your mind is racing as you watch the dark car drive away. You almost can't believe what you've just seen and heard. First a big-money development is about to be approved by the town, when suddenly the only person to oppose the project disappears. Now someone in a fancy car passes a thick envelope to a town councilman.

You drop from the tree back into the parking lot and look around carefully. But the two cars have left no trace of their meeting.

You just watched a payoff, a bribe. You're sure of it. And you were the only witness. You've got to do something, but what?

You decide not to talk to anyone—not even Corey—until you figure out what to do. Walking home in the dark, you come up with three possible courses of action.

Go on to the next page.

You could go to the *Grantshire Observer* and tell the editor what you just heard. Or you could find Andrea Sorrell, the daughter of the missing councilman. If she's come up from New York City, she must suspect something too. Or you could round up Corey and Kate. No one knows this town better than the three of you. Maybe you and your friends could solve this mystery on your own—though right now, you're not sure how.

If you go to the Observer,
turn to page 10.

*If you try to find Andrea Sorrell,
turn to page 28.*

*If you round up your friends,
turn to page 71.*

Andrea's penlight lights up a slice of a page under "B."

"Belleville Transport," you read. "Office and main depot, Old Bridge Road, Grantshire. Storage warehouse, Devil's Ditch Road, Woodard's Mill."

Andrea checks the wall map again. "My father's fishing camp is not far from the road to Woodard's Mill. They could have grabbed him at the camp and taken him to this warehouse."

"But where's Devil's Ditch Road?"

"We'll find it," she says. "Let's go!"

But when you arrive at the back door you're just in time to see the Belleville truck roar to life. Spitting gravel, the truck spins out of the lot, heading away from town.

Only then do you realize that Corey is gone.

Turn to page 89.

"I know how we can do it," Corey says. "We'll call one of our conspirators on his car phone. After all, we're reporters, right? We'll ask questions, and meanwhile Kate can work her scanner until she finds the frequency."

"Great idea," you say. "Then Kate's scanner can pick up every call the guy makes. We'll crack the conspiracy wide open."

"Only one problem," says Kate. "Cellular phones are private. Only the owner can give out his number."

Corey shrugs. "Let's ask Lew Millman." He goes to a pay phone nearby. You see him dial, speak for a moment, then scribble a note. Then he's back. "He doesn't know Strassen's number. The guy doesn't trust the press, remember? But Collins talks to everyone. I have his number right here."

"We could call him," you say. "He likes to talk. But this other guy, Strassen, is the main conspirator. How can we get his number?"

"Why don't we ask him for it?" Corey says. "The town council is voting on the mall tonight, right? I bet Strassen's going to be there. We show up a little early, and when Strassen's about to go into the meeting, we ask to interview him. He won't want to talk to us right then—he'll be in a big hurry. So we'll ask to call him tomorrow."

Go on to the next page.

"It could work," you say slowly.

"Of course it could," says Corey. "Why would he be suspicious of three kids?"

"I don't know," says Kate. "It sounds like a lot of trouble when we could just call this Collins guy instead." She looks at you. "What do you think we should do?"

If you suggest calling Councilman Collins, turn to page 90.

If you decide to approach Strassen, turn to page 16.

Marvin Turner, the Grantshire police chief, is working late. He lets you into the station himself. Sitting at his desk, he listens to your story while he sips a diet cola. When you've finished he sets down the can and leans back in his chair.

"An envelope that you claim you saw—that's not evidence," says the chief. "You don't know who the councilman was talking to. You don't know what was in the envelope. You can't even prove it was the councilman there in the first place."

"But I saw his face. Can't you question him?"

Chief Turner shakes his head. "I am not going to accuse a prominent Grantshire citizen of corruption when the only evidence I have is something that a child claims to have seen."

You're furious. A *child!*

As you're leaving the police station, you glance through the chief's office window. He has picked up his phone and is dialing a number.

While you ride home, you wonder who he was calling. Could he be in on this plot, too?

Turn to page 18.

54

You decide to stay in the truck. For now, there's nothing to do but feel around the dark, empty cargo area. Carefully, quietly, you cover the whole space. Your hands sweep the dirty floor. You reach into corners. Your fingers feel every inch.

You find that plywood sheeting is bolted all around the bottom four feet of the truck sides to keep cargo from sliding into the metal. You feel along the top of the plywood. Your fingers find something—a few small sheets of thin, odd-feeling paper. They've been folded and stuck between the plywood sheeting and the wall. You slip the papers into your pocket.

After some time, the truck pulls over and stops. You grab the burlap and pull it back over your face. A moment later the gate rolls up and you're lifted roughly by the arms and hauled outside.

Your captors don't say a word. They tie your hands together, then your feet. Then their footsteps crunch away.

The truck roars back to life and pulls away, leaving you blindfolded, tied up, and alone.

Turn to page 113.

It's getting dark. As you ride up Coolidge, the central street in Grantshire, you switch on your new light. Several blocks to the north, you pull over and wait.

It's a quiet summer night. Not many cars are on the streets. You finger the two-way radio.

You don't have to wait long.

The handset crackles. "He's getting in his car," says Kate. "Stay tuned. He's pulling out."

You're ready to move. If Strassen turns south toward Corey, you and Kate will follow as fast as you can. If he comes north toward you, Corey and Kate will ride your way. And you'll hope Strassen goes straight past, so you can get on his tail.

"He's turning," Kate says. "He's going north!"

"I'm on my way," Corey's voice crackles. "Stay with him!"

You pull your bike a few feet off the street so Strassen won't see you. A few seconds later, his familiar dark car cruises by.

You pull onto Coolidge and pedal hard. Strassen isn't driving very fast, but his car is outpacing your bike, and the gap is widening. You ride as fast as you can. Parked cars and side streets slip past quickly.

Up ahead, you see Strassen signal for a right turn. You peer up at the street sign as he turns: Parson Street. Suddenly you realize where the meeting is going to be.

Turn to page 101.

Inside, about twenty-five people are sitting on folding chairs in a square room lit with fluorescent lights. At the front, six town council members sit at a long table.

Kate nudges you. "Which one's Collins?"

"At the far right," you say.

The only woman on the council, sitting at the center, bangs a dark wooden gavel to open the meeting. "She must be the president," you whisper. You look around and see that Strassen is sitting alone on the other side of the room.

"Before we vote on the Maple Grove Mall proposal," says the council president, "would any members of the public like to comment?"

A young, neatly dressed woman stands up. "I would," she says. She sounds a little nervous. "I'm unemployed right now," she tells the council. "I worked for six years downtown as a salesclerk, but then I got laid off. We need this mall in town. People need jobs." She sits down.

"Anyone else?" the council president asks.

"I've got something to say," says an older man wearing a plaid hunting jacket. "I've lived in this town all my life—but I've been around, too," the man says. "I've seen what these big shopping malls have done to other towns. If we let this mall in, no one will shop in town anymore. The downtown stores will close. Why should we let some out-of-state corporation drive our local people out of business?"

The man sits down. You see Collins shoot Strassen a nervous glance.

Turn to page 31.

The carbons show a Belleville trucker's signature. When the state police locate him and inform him they are going to charge him with kidnapping, the trucker tells them the whole story—how Cairo bought Belleville Transport and used its trucks to kidnap Frank Sorrell and then you. The scheme unravels from there.

The state cops find Frank Sorrell in a Belleville storage warehouse thirty miles away in Woodard's Mill. He gives Vermont State Police detectives the evidence he's been collecting.

The Cairo Corporation people are in real trouble. They face two counts of kidnapping and six counts of bribing a public official. Plus the police chief and three town council members are charged with accepting bribes. It's awful news for Grantshire, but it would be a lot worse to have Cairo Corporation running your whole town.

Turn to page 5.

"Let's play it safe and stick to the speed limit," you tell Andrea. "It'll give us time to come up with a plan."

"All right," she says. She eases the sports car down to fifty-five.

While the car hums along, you study the atlas map of Woodard's Mill. "Devil's Ditch Road is a couple of miles outside the village," you say. "Looks like a quiet location for a warehouse."

"That'd be a real plus if you were hiding something—or someone," says Andrea.

You nod. "Here comes Route 74." The car swings easily into the right turn. You glance at Andrea. "We can't just cruise up to the warehouse," you say. "If they're there, they'll hear us coming. They might even have a lookout."

"I was just thinking that too," she says. "I wonder if—hey! What's that?"

She slows down and pulls to a quick stop at the roadside. Just ahead, in some bushes, you see a pale shape. It's moving.

"Is it some kind of animal?" Andrea asks.

"I don't know. It looks pretty big." You flick on your penlight and gasp. "It's Corey!"

Turn to page 78.

60

You approach the dumpster nervously.

"Give me a boost, okay?" you whisper to Corey.

You place your foot in his cupped hands, push yourself up, and look in. To your dismay, the dumpster is nearly full.

"Oh well," you sigh. "Here goes." You pull yourself over the rim and tumble in.

Your sneakers land on something slippery and soft. Your left leg is wet. Suddenly you hear a funny beeping sound coming from the parking lot. You peek over the rim of the dumpster. You see a pair of red taillights glowing as a garbage truck backs in.

Stunned, you wonder for an instant what to do. If you jump out, the truck may not see you. You could be crushed. The truck is only a few yards away by now.

Something moves above the truck, and you see Kate swing down on the branch and drop into the parking lot. She's trying to stop the truck, but it's backing up too fast. The truck's left rear corner smacks her full in the chest. She crumples to the pavement—and the truck keeps backing up.

Turn to page 81.

You're bounced around on the metal floor as the vehicle picks up speed. When it takes a turn you're sent tumbling into the side, the cloth still tied tight around your face.

You realize that you must be in the back of that Belleville truck. You seem to be alone back here. As scared as you are, you remember that after you were heaved in, you heard the rear door roll down—yet you didn't hear it click.

But first things first.

Luckily your hands are not tied. You pull at the heavy, itchy burlap over your face. You feel a thick knot at the back. You work the cloth patiently upward, and finally it comes loose.

The air inside the truck is hot and musty. The truck's motion sways you as you crawl softly, carefully, through the dark to the rear of the vehicle, where you can see a thin glimmer of moonlight at the bottom of the rear gate. You were right—they didn't latch it!

You could try to lift the gate, hoping that the driver won't hear you. Then you could jump out the back of the truck and escape. But you're not sure where you are—and you could get hurt. Maybe it would be better to stay in here and try to learn who the kidnappers are. You might even be able to find out where they've taken Frank Sorrell.

If you try to escape, turn to page 95.

If you stay in the truck, turn to page 54.

At the front of the room, six town council members sit at a long table. Art Collins is at one end. The council president is sitting in the middle, holding a gavel. She's about to bang it onto the table.

"If no one else wishes to speak," she says into a microphone, "we'll vote on the Maple Grove Mall proposal."

You open your mouth, but you're speechless. You take a step forward.

For an instant the council president looks at you and raises her eyebrows. You take a step backward and lurch back out through the double doors.

Out in the hall, breathing hard, you hear the gavel bang.

No evidence, you think, as the council inside votes to approve the Maple Grove Mall. I just didn't have any evidence.

The End

You inch along the wall until you're only a few feet from the rear of the truck. The guard is on the other side.

You quietly lower yourself to the ground, crawl to the truck, and slide beneath it. On your belly beneath the rear wheels, you can see the guard's feet. You pull out your penlight and aim it downstream, flashing it once.

Corey is watching for your signal. The second he sees it, he's supposed to turn away from the warehouse, point his light toward Andrea, and flash it once, his body shielding his signal from the lookout's view.

A second later you hear a car approaching. The sound of the powerful engine grows louder, and the guard's feet move as he turns to watch. You draw out your pocketknife and unfold the blade.

As Andrea's car roars by, you plunge the knife into the sidewall of the truck's left rear tire. The sound of the car's engine covers the hissing escape of air.

Meanwhile Andrea has turned the car and is accelerating back down the road. The lookout rushes inside just before the car zooms past. You know that she's on her way to the nearby village to call the police. You turn and crawl to the edge of the truck. You're about to break for the stream when the warehouse door is flung open and two men come out, dragging a third man, who is bound and gagged. You freeze. It must be Frank Sorrell!

Turn to page 88.

"Not exactly," says Ted. "You see, all calls by cellular phone in each twenty-five-mile area are handled by one 'cell,' or relay tower. That cell uses one slice of the radio spectrum—say, an inch on your dial. When a call comes through, the tower transmits it on a frequency within that slice."

"Okay. I can keep checking the frequencies across that slice," says Kate. "Wouldn't I pick up the person's calls then?"

"Probably," says Ted. "In a country area like this there aren't very many cellular calls. But you'd be invading the person's privacy. It's not illegal to listen to the radio, but some people might not appreciate it."

"Maybe not," says Kate. "But if someone is using a cellular phone to manage a criminal conspiracy—that's worse, right?"

"Well, yeah. Using the airwaves for illegal activity is a federal offense. Very serious stuff." Ted studies Kate closely. "What's going on, anyway?"

"Oh . . ." Kate begins.

"We're making up a story," says Corey. "We're writing a play for school."

Ted grins again. "Getting a jump on next school year, eh? Well, good luck."

The three of you say good-bye to Ted and leave the store. "Somehow," says Kate, "we've got to get one of these guys talking on his cellular phone, so we can find that frequency range."

Turn to page 50.

Changing a truck's tire is hard work. It takes the two men at least fifteen minutes. To you, flattened against the building a few feet away, it seems like half the night. You wonder if Andrea has found a phone. Somewhere nearby in the woods, Corey is waiting, just as helpless as you are.

Finally the job is finished. The men fling the old tire aside, jump back into the cab, and pull out onto Devil's Ditch Road.

Your body sags. They're going to make it. After all that!

The truck starts down the road. Stepping out after it, you flash your light toward Corey. Peering into the woods, you see his answering flash. And then you see another, different kind of light —the flashing blue light of a Vermont state police cruiser! It's coming up Devil's Ditch Road, heading straight toward the Belleville truck.

A siren goes on, and you whoop with joy. You did it!

The End

"I guess you'd better keep speeding," you tell Andrea. "We've got to catch up to that truck."

"You got it," Andrea says. The high-powered car continues to hum along the curvy road as if it's riding on rails. You'd hardly know you were going seventy-five miles an hour. In the darkness you glide past a farmhouse and two barns. Suddenly you spot a car parked along the shoulder of the road.

"Uh-oh," you say. You turn and see that the car is pulling onto the road and speeding after you. A second later a siren begins to wail and blue police lights flash on the car's roof.

Andrea sighs. As she pulls the car off the road, she says to you, "It's okay—just a ticket. We'll be rolling again in five minutes."

You watch the car pull to a stop behind you. You can see the officer inside talking on his radio. After a long minute, he steps out and approaches Andrea's car. But instead of coming over to the window, he steps back and puts his hand on the heel of his gun.

"Open the door slowly, please," he tells Andrea. "You are under arrest."

Turn to page 34.

"All right, let's follow that car," you say. You and Corey grab your bikes and hit the road. You pedal as hard as you can, but by the time you round the bend, there's no sign of the car.

But as you continue toward town, the dark car suddenly passes you from behind. It glides by very slowly and stops just in front of you. The driver's door opens and the blond-haired man steps out. He stands by the car and looks straight at you as you pedal by. His look is hard and cold. You feel a chill of fear crawl down your back.

Turn to page 33.

You, Corey, and Kate have tackled plenty of problems together in the past. You decide to enlist their help with this mystery.

The next morning you meet them at the old ballpark. The three of you sit beneath a clump of birch trees and gaze out at the weedy lot as you tell them the whole story.

"You're sure that's what you heard?" Corey asks.

"Positive."

"How do you know the guy in the white car was a town councilman?" asks Kate.

"Because I recognized him," you say. "I got a good look at him. It was Collins, I'm sure of it."

"Okay, say something illegal *is* going on," Corey says. "What can we do about it?"

"We can get evidence," you say. "Real, solid evidence."

"How?" asks Kate.

You study your friends. Corey's the quick thinker in your little group, the one you want with you in a tight spot. Kate has a real talent for technology; she's a whiz with any gadget she can get her hands on.

"We can do it," you say, "but we need a strategy. So let's think. What do we know so far?"

Turn to page 111.

"What is it?" you ask.

"Well," Corey says, "wouldn't you like to find out more about Collins and this dark-car guy? Maybe we can really get the goods on them."

"How?" asks Kate.

"We do a story on the mall for the *Grantshire Observer,*" Corey says. "That'll let us ask questions without getting anyone suspicious."

"But why would the paper let three kids be reporters?"

Corey grins. "Kids in town want to know about this mall, right? So why shouldn't the town paper want a story about the mall from the kids' point of view?"

"It's not a bad idea," says Kate. "Except for one thing. If these guys pass their final bribe tomorrow night and we don't witness it, we might lose our one big chance to catch them in the act."

"That's true, I guess," Corey says. He turns to you. "What do you think? Should we just stake out the parking lot tomorrow night or try to become investigative reporters?"

*If you decide to stake out the parking lot,
turn to page 102.*

*If you want to try to become reporters,
turn to page 82.*

It turns out to be your last conscious act. You sail through the air until your head smacks on a stone and you tumble into a shallow ditch. It's cool here. The lonely country road fades to a soft blur . . .

Lying a little below the road level, half submerged in water, your body isn't spotted for several days. Andrea Sorrell tries desperately to convince the authorities that you were kidnapped. But she's told there's no evidence. Your death remains a mystery.

In your memory, the new Maple Grove Mall is renamed—after you.

The End

The next day, the three of you wait until mid-morning. Then you go to the phone in Kate's kitchen and dial the number Strassen gave you. A woman's voice answers. "Hello, Grantshire Inn," she says. "How may I direct your call?"

"Oh, ah," you mumble, "I must have the wrong number. Sorry." You hang up. "Rats—it's the inn," you say.

"That must be where he's staying," says Corey.

"So we're sunk," Kate moans.

"Not necessarily," Corey says. "Maybe we can't do the car-phone thing. But we know Collins and Strassen are meeting tonight for the big payoff."

"The question is when," says Kate. "And where."

"When is probably right around nine—that's when they did it last time," you say. "Right after dark. *Where* is tougher."

"We could stake out the lot behind Grantshire Market," Kate suggests. "Maybe they'll go there again."

"I bet they won't," says Corey. "Too risky to meet at the same spot twice."

"Why? They don't know anybody's onto them," you argue.

Go on to the next page.

"We could try to tail Strassen tonight instead," Corey says. "You know, follow him. One of us waits outside the inn. We have a system of signals—we could use walkie-talkies. It might not work, but then again it might. If we go to the market and they don't come there, we've lost our chance." He shrugs. "But the choice is up to you."

If you stake out Grantshire Market,
turn to page 102.

If you try to tail Strassen,
turn to page 104.

That Thursday the photo you took is spread across the front page of the *Grantshire Observer*. Above it is the headline:

COUNCILMAN CAUGHT IN BRIBERY SCHEME
MALL PLAN WAS CORE OF CORRUPTION

In the newspaper's crammed and messy office, Lew Millman hands you and your friends some extra copies.

"The FBI picked up Collins and Strassen last night," he tells you. "They're about to announce some more arrests. I'm off to cover it." He heads out the door, then stops. "You three did an incredible job," he says. "I guess you'll be heroes in school."

"I bet we won't," you say. "A lot of kids really wanted that mall."

"Well, personally, I'm glad to see the Cairo Corporation run out of town," Millman says. "And I promise you, the *Grantshire Observer* will get that scraggly lot turned into a proper ballpark."

"Can we do a story about it?" you ask.

"Are you kidding? You three are the best reporters I've ever had!"

The End

You and Andrea jump out of the car and rush to untie the strips of burlap that blindfold your friend's face and bind his hands and feet.

Corey blinks. "I don't know how you found me," he says hoarsely, "but I'm sure glad you did."

"Come on," you say. "Quick!"

The three of you hurry back to the car. Andrea starts the engine and steers back onto the road. "How far ahead are they?" she asks Corey.

"Five minutes," Corey says from his perch in the tiny backseat. "No more."

"Did you get a look at them?"

"No. They grabbed me from behind and threw me in back of the truck. Then they stopped to dump me in that bush. I think it was two guys."

"Did they say anything?" Andrea asks.

"Yeah," says Corey quietly. "When they were climbing back into the truck, I heard one of them say, 'Let's go take care of the old guy.'"

Turn to page 92.

80

"We may not have much time," you tell your friends. The three of you straddle a low branch of the tree so that you're overlooking the parking lot.

There's not much to see down there except a dark green dumpster. Behind it is a pile of large cardboard boxes.

"One of us should hide in those boxes," you decide.

"Yuck," says Kate. "I'm not going in those slimy things."

"Okay, then you get the even tastier choice," you say.

"Which is?"

You smile and point to the dumpster.

"Forget it," says Kate. "No conspiracy is worth that."

"All right, all right," you answer. "Kate, you stay up here. Corey, you hide in the boxes. I'll take the dumpster."

"Okay. Let's hustle then," says Corey. "The bad guys could arrive any minute."

You and Corey drop into the parking lot as Kate slips back into the branches.

Turn to page 60.

"Kate!" you scream. "Hey—stop!" But the beeping noise drowns out your voice.

Just then a second figure dashes out from behind the dumpster. It's Corey. He runs and flings himself up on the truck's running board and pounds on the driver's door.

The truck stops. You heave yourself over the rim of the dumpster and drop to the ground. Kate is lying motionless two inches from the truck's huge rear tire.

Corey and the driver come running around the truck. They crouch beside you.

"Kate," you whisper. "Kate!" There's no answer.

The trucker places a large hand gently on your friend's temple. "She's got a good pulse. She's breathing okay. But she's out."

He stands up. "I'll radio for the rescue squad. They'll be here in two minutes. She'll be okay. What were you kids doing back here anyway?"

Turn to page 93.

"Let's go with Corey's idea," you say. "Being reporters could be fun."

The three of you ride downtown and approach the office of the *Grantshire Observer*. Paint is peeling off the outside walls.

"This building could use a wrecking ball," Corey comments.

Just then the screen door clatters open. A balding man rushes out, stuffing a mess of papers into a canvas shoulder bag. You try to step aside but he isn't watching where he's going and you both sprawl to the grass, the papers scattering all over.

"Oh no—my ad sheets!" The man lunges after them. Corey and Kate chase the papers that are fluttering off in the breeze.

"Sorry about that," you say.

"Hey, it's my fault. Too much to do—I forget to look. Were you coming to see me?"

"We were hoping to see the editor of the newspaper."

"That's me. Lew Millman—editor, reporter, publisher, and right now, advertising salesman." He shakes hands with each of you.

"Mr. Millman," says Corey, "all the kids in town are talking about the plans for the new mall. They want to know what the mall would have for young people."

Go on to page 84.

84

"That's a good question," Millman says. "Maybe I could do a story."

"Maybe we could do it for you," says Kate.

Millman scratches his head. "Not a bad idea," he says. "I can't pay you anything, but if you come up with a good story, I'll print it."

"Great," you say. "Can you give us some background information?"

Turn to page 26.

At twenty minutes before seven, you park your bike outside the town hall. Kate's tiny cassette recorder is taped inside your sweatshirt. A wire runs from the machine through a hole in your shirt to a very small "bead" microphone pinned to your chest behind a large Boston Red Sox button.

You're feeling nervous, but you force yourself to breathe steadily. You reach under your sweatshirt and push the machine's Record button. As you start to walk toward the building, you stop short. Art Collins's white car is parked just a few feet away, and he's sitting inside! What if he saw you reach under your shirt?

Though your heart is pounding, you try to act casual as you stroll toward the white car. As you get closer, you see that Collins isn't paying any attention to you—he's talking on his car phone.

Taking a deep breath, you tap on the car window. Collins hangs up and rolls down the window.

"Hello there, youngster," he says. "What can I do for you?"

"Well sir," you say, "I'd really like to get a job at the Grantshire Market. Aren't you the manager there?"

Collins scratches his head. "Why, no. I sell shoes for a living."

"Oh, gosh, sorry. But I saw you drive out from behind the building last night. Weren't you closing up the market?"

Turn to page 20.

You arrive at Radio Cave, a local electronics store, a few minutes later. A rumpled-looking young man with an impish face steps out of the back room. "Hey, Kate!" he says with a grin.

"This is Ted," Kate says to you and Corey. "Ted's my technical consultant."

"All Things Technoid, that's me," says Ted. "What're you into this time, Kate?"

"Ted, is it possible to intercept a cellular phone's transmission?" she asks.

"Well, yes. A cellular phone is a radio, transmitting on a radio frequency. You'd need a good wideband receiver. But you've got one of those, right?"

"Yes. How could you find a particular phone's signal?"

Ted frowns. "I guess you'd just have to search," he says. "If the caller had a distinctive voice, maybe you could do it. One thing, though—the other side of a cellular conversation comes in on a slightly different frequency. You'd only be able to hear the one person talking, not both like on a regular phone."

"Hmm," says Kate. "But once you found a person's frequency, you could monitor everything that was said from that phone, right?"

Turn to page 66.

Frank Sorrell's bound feet scrape on the ground as the two men drag him toward the truck's rear door. Now his feet are just inches from your face as you lie beneath the truck. The feet move, and Sorrell stands up. He's alive!

The men heave Sorrell into the truck. You hold your breath. What if they notice the flat tire now?

Sorrell's body tumbles onto the metal floor just above you. The kidnappers haul down the back gate and rush toward the cab.

"Hey, it could have been a local hot-rodder," says one.

"That was a foreign sports car," the other replies. "It was no local. Let's roll."

The truck's engine roars to life. It clunks into gear and lunges forward, clanking and jerking on its airless tires. You've got to move, even though they might see you.

Exposed, you hunch over and run to the building's back wall. You press your back tightly against the wall as the truck stops, the doors open, and the two men leap out.

Dashing to the rear, the men curse. "What a time for *this* to happen," says one.

"Let's just change it—fast," the other says.

Barely daring to breathe, you stay flat against the building. Just six feet away, the two men work feverishly to change the tire. What if they notice that the tire has been deliberately cut and decide to search the lot?

Turn to page 67.

"They've got Corey!" you exclaim.

"I know," Andrea says grimly. "I never should have gotten you kids into this."

"They turned away from Grantshire—toward Woodard's Mill," you say. "We've got to follow them."

A few seconds later you reach Andrea's speedy dark green sports car. "Get in," she says. She flips you a brand-new copy of *The Vermont Atlas and Gazetteer*. It's got detailed maps, showing roads and rivers—even tiny lanes and narrow streams—for every piece of Vermont.

"I just bought this," she says. "Thought I might need it. What's the fastest way to Woodard's Mill?"

"Head straight down route 7," you say. You're thumbing for the right page. "Then, let's see . . ."

You're slammed back against your seat as the powerful car takes off.

Turn to page 15.

90

The next morning you and your friends prepare to telephone Councilman Collins from Kate's basement. Though you are disturbed by the town council's vote of the previous evening to approve the Maple Grove Mall, you are determined to press on with your investigation.

The air in Kate's basement is cool. The walls are lined with knotty pine paneling. On a bumper-pool table in the middle of the room Kate has set up a piece of plywood that holds a wideband radio receiver and a small cassette tape recorder. Next to the recorder is a small toggle switch.

After checking the equipment Kate turns on her stool and takes off her headphones. "I'm ready," she says. "Go up and call."

You and Corey walk up the wooden stairs while Kate puts the headphones back on. You pick up the phone in Kate's kitchen. Corey sits beside you with a list of questions. A small homemade box that holds a flashlight bulb is sitting on the counter beside you. A wire runs from the box down the basement stairs.

When you dial the number for Collins's cellular car phone, a gravelly, cheerful voice answers, "Yeah!"

"Hello, Mr. Collins?"

"That's me. Who's this?"

You tell him your name. "Mr. Collins, I'm doing a story for the *Grantshire Observer* about the Maple Grove Mall. I'd like my story to answer the questions that kids in town are asking."

Turn to page 12.

Andrea's hands clench the wheel. "Dad!" she whispers. She stomps the gas pedal, and the car rockets down the country road.

"You know, these guys are dangerous," Corey says. "Maybe we should find a pay phone and call the state police."

"By the time a state cruiser gets to the warehouse, that truck—and my dad—could be long gone," Andrea answers.

"Not if we can hold them up a while," you say. You're studying the map. "I've got an idea."

Turn to page 44.

"Oh," you answer. "We were just . . ."

"Dumpster diving," says Corey.

The trucker looks confused. "Dumpster diving?"

"Yeah," says Corey. "You know, looking for good stuff."

"Oh, great," says the driver as he walks to his cab. "This is going to make my job real interesting."

As the driver radios for help, you look at Corey. "Dumpster diving?" you say. "How do you think of these things?"

Corey smiles and shrugs. "It's a talent, I guess."

You shake your head. "I guess we don't have much of a talent for crime solving, though."

"Maybe we should tell the police what you saw," Corey suggests.

"This is too big for the Grantshire cops," you answer. "Tomorrow morning we're going to call the FBI."

Corey whistles. "OK," he says, "but you do the talking."

"Don't worry," you say with a smile. You're a bit nervous, but you can't wait to make that call.

The End

"But paying off a town council member is against the law," you tell the editor. "That's a big story!"

"It would be, if you could prove it," Lew Millman says. "But you've got no evidence—it'd be your word against Mr. Collins's. Besides, the people at the Cairo Corporation stand to make a lot of money from building this mall. They aren't about to let us stop them."

"What's the Cairo Corporation?"

"The developer. They're a nationwide corporation that comes into towns like this one, buys up empty lots, and builds big malls. Some people say they're ruthless. If I tried to stop them, they could put my paper out of business. I don't know what they'd do to you. If I were you I'd just forget what you saw."

You turn to leave. "Thanks for the information," you say.

"Sure," says the editor. As you walk out, he calls out after you. "Hey, I thought all you kids were excited about the mall!"

You turn back. "Malls are cool," you answer. "But bribing one council member and maybe kidnapping another—that's not."

Turn to page 13.

You ease the truck's rear gate open inch by inch. When it's almost high enough, the truck hits a pothole and you're heaved into the wall with a loud *thunk*.

The truck slows down. You hold your breath. The driver seems to hesitate. But a moment later the truck roars forward again. You let out your breath, then resume inching the gate up.

Finally the opening is high enough for you to slip through. You decide to wait until the truck slows down for a curve. Finally you feel the driver downshift, and the truck body sways to the left. Hoping you'll land somewhere soft, you take another breath, close your eyes, and pitch your shoulder into the air.

Turn to page 73.

You wrap up the interview, and then the waiting begins. You and Corey head back downstairs. Kate is putting away the wideband receiver and setting up a modern scanner. She sets it to search a section of the dial around Collins's frequency. For hours you and Corey lounge around, listening, while Kate sits ready to flick the cassette machine to Record.

You hear several cellular phone calls, but none made by Collins. More hours pass. You flip through magazine after magazine. You're beginning to think this isn't going to work when suddenly you hear Collins's voice say, "Hello, Mr. Strassen. Good to hear from you."

Kate starts the recorder. "Bingo," she whispers.

"Right. Tonight," Collins says. "Eleven. Sure. Where? Parson and Coolidge, by the lot, got it. I'll come on foot. That's fine. See you then."

There's a click as Collins hangs up. Kate switches off the recorder. "Parson Street and Coolidge—that's the edge of the old ballpark," she says.

"Guess we know that terrain," Corey adds. "What next?"

Turn to page 106.

"What could it mean?" Corey asks Andrea. "Why would the Cairo Corporation buy a dinky local company like Belleville Transport?"

"Here's my theory," she says. "Cairo has been paying off the town council and the police and who knows who else to get its plans approved. But my dad wouldn't cooperate. Frank Sorrell served forty-five years in the New York Police Department and never took a bribe. I bet he was putting together the evidence to show just how much power the Cairo Corporation's money has bought in this town. I think he was 'disappeared.' "

"You mean killed?"

Andrea's face pales. "I hope not," she says. "I hope he's just been kidnapped. But we've got to move fast. I'd like to find out what trucks left Belleville Transport on the day my dad disappeared and where they were going. That means visiting Belleville late tonight."

You glance at Corey, who nods. "We want to help you," you tell Andrea.

She looks doubtful. "I don't know . . ." she begins.

"You need our help," Corey insists. "We know this town better than anyone."

Go on to the next page.

"Well," Andrea says slowly. "You have a point. Since I'm a stranger in town it would be helpful to have a guide." She looks at the two of you seriously. "But you have to promise me you'll be careful and not put yourselves in any danger."

You and Corey nod.

Turn to page 19.

100

The two men shove through the bushes in pursuit. You hear them pounding after you as you head for the opening between two clumps of birches. Reaching the opening, you hop slightly. So do your friends.

The two men are right behind you now. Sprinting desperately, they reach the opening—and the dark wire you've strung between the twin clumps of trees.

You hear sharp cries of pain as the men hit the ground hard. They howl and curse as you and your friends disappear into a grove of trees.

You veer apart and sprint along well-known paths as planned, each of you going a separate way. You come out on Coolidge Avenue and dash across. Reaching the buildings on the other side, you turn quickly. Dashing behind an auto-repair shop, you cross the train tracks and hop a fence. Soon you're back in your own familiar neighborhood.

A few minutes later you're lifting the metal door that leads from Kate's backyard to her basement. Already waiting in the darkness down below, Corey grins up at you.

A moment later you hear Kate's running sneakers. You lift the door, and she climbs down. "I guess you got it," she says to you.

You hold up the camera. "Sure did."

She pulls a cassette out of her pocket and smiles. "So did I."

Turn to page 77.

Parson Street is a nearly deserted road on the way out of town. Almost the only thing on it is the empty lot—the old ballpark. That must be where Strassen and Collins are planning to make the payoff!

You're gasping for breath now, riding harder than you ever have in your life. Your bike's light casts a glow on the darkening avenue. You don't know how far back Corey and Kate are, but you hope they get here fast—Kate has the camera!

Finally you reach the corner of Coolidge and Parson. You can just see the red taillights of Strassen's car slowing down beside the big empty lot a couple of hundred feet away. He pulls over and stops.

You turn and look behind you. Way down Coolidge, you see two wavering lights—Kate and Corey. But they're still so far away that it's going to take them several minutes to get here.

You peer down Parson. You don't see another car, but a moment later a man emerges from a nearby abandoned building and crosses the street to walk toward the parked car.

It's Collins. The payoff is about to happen. What should you do? If Kate arrives in time, she can snap the picture that will provide crucial evidence. But she may be too late!

Turn to page 37.

"Let's go for the stakeout," you say. "That seems like our best shot."

At the appointed time, just before 9:00 P.M., you, Corey, and Kate meet in Corey's backyard.

"All the lights are still on at the market," you report. "But it should be getting ready to close."

"Let's hope we're lucky and they show up," Kate says.

"Not lucky—smart," Corey says. "I think we should each pick a hiding place that'll get us close enough to see and hear what goes on."

"The lights went off in the market," you interrupt. "Let's get into position."

Without another word, all three of you swing up into the apple tree.

Turn to page 80.

"All right, let's try to tail him," you say. You spend the rest of the day making plans. You head over to the inn at about eight o'clock that evening to start keeping watch while Kate gets some equipment together. Just before 9:00 P.M. Corey and Kate come riding up to your lookout post across the street from the inn's parking lot. Kate is carrying a small backpack stuffed full of equipment.

"What's the word?" says Corey.

"He's in there," you say. "His car hasn't moved."

"Good," says Kate, getting off her bike. The three of you move into the darkened doorway of a shop that's closed for the night.

Kate opens her pack and pulls out three small two-way radio handsets. "Everybody's got the light on their bikes," she says. "Right?"

"Right," you and Corey reply. Newly bolted onto your handlebars is a battery-powered headlight, with On/Off and flasher switches. Corey has one too.

"Here," says Kate. "These walkie-talkies are small enough to fit in our pockets. They've got a range of up to a mile."

Go on to the next page.

"Right," you say. "Kate, you wait here. When Strassen leaves, he's got to head toward Coolidge. From there, he has to turn either south toward the market or north toward Route 7. Corey, you ride four or five blocks south on Coolidge. I'll go a few blocks north. Kate, as soon as you see Strassen move, get on the radio."

"I will," says Kate. "I've got the camera in my backpack."

"Can't forget that," you say. "Okay. Let's move."

Turn to page 55.

Kate walks over to a wall of metal shelves crammed with gadgets. She pulls out a long-handled microphone and a camera with a built-in flash. "Corey," she says, "this is a telescope mike. It'll pick up a conversation up to twenty-five feet away. You use it, and I'll run the cassette recorder." She hands you the camera. "You get the dangerous job."

You nod. To get the proof you need, you're going to have to take at least one picture. And that'll mean using the flash.

Turn to page 39.

You twist around and see that the person who grabbed you is Grantshire's chief of police, Marvin Turner. Despite his heft, the chief has snuck up behind you silently. He's got one big hand on each of you. You spot his cruiser parked farther down the road.

"I know kids get bored with swimming and squirt-gun fights late in the summer," he says. "But why spy on a trucking company?"

"Um," you stammer, "well, Chief, we . . ." You don't want to tell him the truth.

"Trucks!" Corey interrupts. "We love trucks!"

Chief Turner smiles broadly. "Ah," he says, letting go of you and Corey. "I used to like trucks too. Still, this is private property."

"But Chief," you say, "we're not on their property."

Chief Turner's face grows stern. "Listen, kids. I'm telling you not to hang around this place. If I see you here again I'm going to have to cart you home and speak with your folks. This is your warning." He walks back to his patrol car.

"What do you think he was doing?" Corey muses when the chief is out of earshot. "Just patroling?"

"Maybe," you say thoughtfully. "Or maybe he was giving Belleville Transport some extra attention." Suddenly you see a flash of movement out of the corner of your eye. You turn and see that the blond-haired man is emerging from Belleville's office. You and Corey duck behind the tree again and watch.

Turn to page 32.

Following Corey, you soon discover that he knows this neighborhood well enough to know that there's a deep ditch running between the backyards of the houses. "Keep your head down and follow me," he whispers.

A few minutes later, you and Corey poke your heads above the rim of the ditch.

"That's the place," Corey says, nodding at a white clapboard house with dark green shutters.

You notice that the lawn has grown scraggly in the days since Sorrell has been missing. "I bet that's a sign he didn't take off on his own," you whisper. "Most people would arrange to have someone cut their lawn while they were away."

Corey nods. Then he elbows you and points to the house's kitchen window. There is a woman inside, looking out at you. She disappears from sight for a moment. Then the back door opens, just a little.

Ducking from one well-trimmed shrub to another, you and Corey make your way up to the house. The back door opens, and you slip inside.

"I'm Andrea Sorrell," says the woman who let you in. She is tall and attractive, about thirty years old, with black hair.

You introduce yourselves. "Ms. Sorrell," you say, "we think there's something funny about this mall project."

"So do I," she says. "Come on in and let's talk."

Turn to page 36.

"Let's wait and catch him inside," you say. You follow Strassen into the building and through a pair of double doors into the town council's meeting room. About twenty-five people are there already. The meeting seems to be about to start. You take a deep breath, walk up to Strassen, and tug on the back of his suit jacket.

He turns around and eyes you icily. "Yes?" he says, raising an eyebrow.

"Sorry to bother you, Mr. Strassen," you whisper, "but we're doing a story for the town paper on the mall—from the kids' angle. Can we call you tomorrow for a short interview?"

Strassen glances around. He sees that several people are watching your exchange. Looking irritated, he reaches into his pocket and bends toward you.

"All right," he says. "Call this number." He scribbles a phone number on a scrap of paper and hands it to you.

You nod and smile and back away quickly.

Outside, Corey slaps you on the back. "It worked!" he exclaims.

You nod. "I think he really wanted to tell us to get lost, but he didn't want to do it in front of all those people."

"We'll call him tomorrow," says Kate. "Let's just hope this number is his car phone."

Turn to page 75.

"We know one councilman is missing," says Corey.

"We know Councilman Collins is involved in some sneaky way," says Kate. "We know there's been a passing of envelopes."

"We know there'll be one more pass—the big one," you add.

"Right. We're pretty sure the main guy is the one who drives that long, dark car. We know he met Collins behind the Grantshire Market."

And," you add, "they said they'd make the connection again in the usual way."

"Which probably means behind the Grantshire Market," says Corey. "We could stake it out."

Kate looks excited. "Why not? If all three of us say we saw them, that'd count for something. Right?"

"I guess so," you answer. "But Collins said he'd pick up the final payment 'the night after the vote.' How will we know when that is?"

"I happen to know," says Kate, "that the town council is voting tonight on approving the mall. With that one councilman out of the way, it's a cinch they'll give it the go-ahead."

"How do you *happen* to know that?" you ask.

"I *happen* to read the town newspaper," Kate answers.

"The newspaper," Corey muses. "That gives me another idea."

Turn to page 72.

You think fast. "Let's do it now," you say. "Come on."

You walk toward Strassen. He's carrying a black briefcase and striding toward the door.

"Hello," you say, falling in step beside him, "Mr. Strassen? Hello?"

The man ignores you and keeps walking.

"Mr. Strassen, we're working on a story about the mall for the *Observer*," Kate says.

"A story for kids," Corey puts in.

"Right," you say. "So can we interview you? I mean, not right now—I can see you're in a hurry." Strassen doesn't look down, but you press on as he starts up the steps. "Could we maybe call you? Like tomorrow?"

Finally the man turns toward you. His face is smooth and expressionless. "No," he says.

"But . . ." you begin.

"I do not speak with the press. And don't ask again. I don't like to be pestered."

You stop and watch, openmouthed, as Strassen strides into the town hall.

"What a jerk," says Kate.

"First the guy ignores us," says Corey, "then he tells us to beat it. You know what? So far, being a reporter's just like being a kid."

"That's for sure," says Kate.

"Let's go inside and watch," you say. "We need to know if they approve the mall."

Turn to page 56.

You're scared. You don't know where you are, and you can't get loose. Your wrists and ankles hurt a lot. It is definitely the longest night of your life.

At dawn, a state trooper finds you beneath some bushes. He tells you that you are alongside the road to Woodard's Mill.

Then you remember the scraps of paper in your pocket. You pull them out. It turns out they are bill-of-lading carbons. Truckers carry these bills of lading for every shipment they deliver. A bill of lading is a sheet of paper telling what's in the shipment, with several copies and carbon sheets attached to it. Different copies go to the shipper, the trucker, and whoever gets the shipment.

"I guess the trucker stuck these leftover carbons behind the plywood," you tell the trooper. "It was pure coincidence that I found them."

And what a coincidence: the carbons you are holding break the conspiracy wide open.

Turn to page 58.

You, Corey, and Kate slump over your handlebars.

"We did our best," Corey says.

"I know," you say. "It's okay."

"Why don't we go shoot a picture of Collins?" says Kate.

"What, a man taking a walk? That's nothing," you say.

"Yeah," she says. "Well, we sure came close."

Slowly, the three of you ride back down Coolidge Avenue in the dark summer night.

"You know," you tell your friends, "we make a pretty good team."

"We always did," says Corey. He nods back toward the old ballpark. "I'm going to miss that old place."

"Me, too," says Kate.

"Me three," you add. "See you around the mall."

The End

ABOUT THE AUTHOR

DOUG WILHELM is a free-lance writer and editor. The author of *The Forgotten Planet* in the Choose Your Own Adventure series, he has also written articles for newspapers across the country as well as magazines, newsletters, and Ben and Jerry's ice-cream wrappers. He currently lives in Montpelier, Vermont, and has a son, Bradley, who is six years old.

ABOUT THE ILLUSTRATOR

TOM LA PADULA graduated from Parsons School of Design with a B.F.A. and earned his M.F.A. from Syracuse University.

For over a decade Tom has illustrated for national and international magazines, advertising agencies and publishing houses. Besides his illustrating, Tom is on the faculty of Pratt Institute where he teaches a class in illustration.

During the spring of 1992, his work was exhibited in the group show "The Art of the Baseball Card" at the Baseball Hall of Fame in Cooperstown. In addition, the corporation Johnson and Johnson recently acquired one of Tom's illustrations for their private collection.

Mr. La Padula has illustrated *The Luckiest Day of Your Life* and *Secret of the Dolphins* in the Choose Your Own Adventure series. He resides in New Rochelle, New York, with his wife, son, and daughter.

CHOOSE YOUR OWN ADVENTURE®